Little Raccoon's Nighttime Adventure

By Lilian Moore

Illustrated by Deborah Borgo

Adapted from LITTLE RACCOON AND THE THING IN THE POOL

A GOLDEN BOOK • NEW YORK
Western Publishing Company, Inc., Racine, Wisconsin 53404

Little Raccoon was little
but he was brave.
   One day Mother Raccoon said,
"Tonight the moon will be full.
Can you go to the running stream
all by yourself, Little Raccoon?
Can you bring back some crayfish
for supper?"

"Oh yes, yes!" said Little Raccoon.
"I'll bring back the best crayfish
you ever ate!"
     Little Raccoon was little
but he *was* brave.
     That night his mother said,
"Go now, Little Raccoon.
Walk till you come to the pool."

"You will see a big tree
lying across the pool," she said.
"Walk across the pool on the tree.
The best place to dig for crayfish
is on the other side."
Little Raccoon went off
in the bright moonlight.

He was so happy
and so proud.
Here he was—
walking in the woods
all by himself
for the very first time.
Soon he met Old Porcupine.

"All by yourself?" said Old Porcupine.
"Where are you going?"
   "To get crayfish for supper,"
Little Raccoon said proudly.
   "Be careful, Little Raccoon.
You don't have quills, you know!"
   "I'm not afraid," said Little Raccoon,
and he went on.

Soon he came to the place where
the sweet grass grew.
There was Big Skunk.

"Where are you going, all by yourself?"
he asked.

Little Raccoon told him.

"Be careful," said Big Skunk.
"You can't squirt smells, you know!"

Little Raccoon ran on.
Not far from the running stream
he saw Fat Rabbit.
   "Where are you going all alone,
Little Raccoon?" he asked.
   "Across the pool to dig for crayfish,"
Little Raccoon told him.

"Oooooh!" said Fat Rabbit.
"Aren't you afraid of IT?"
    "Afraid of what?"
asked Little Raccoon.
    "Of the thing in the pool,"
said Fat Rabbit. "I am!"
    "Well, I'm not," said Little Raccoon,
and he ran on.

Soon he came to the tree that was
lying across the pool.
Little Raccoon started to cross.
He did not want to think about
the thing in the pool.
But he just had to stop—
and look down.

Something was looking up at him!
Little Raccoon did not want to show
he was afraid.
So he made a face.
The thing in the pool made a face, too—
a mean face.
Little Raccoon turned and ran.

He did not stop till he saw Big Skunk.
   "What is it? What is it?"
asked Big Skunk.
   "There's a big mean thing in the pool!"
cried Little Raccoon.
   "Take a stone with you," said Big Skunk.
"Show that thing you have a stone!"

Little Raccoon did want to bring home
the crayfish. So he took a stone
and walked back to the pool.
Little Raccoon looked down into the
water, and held up his stone.
The thing in the pool held up
a stone, too—a big stone.

Little Raccoon was brave
but he *was* little.
He ran and ran and he did not stop
till he saw Old Porcupine.
He told him about the thing in the pool.
 "He had a big stone, too!"
said Little Raccoon.

"Go back with a stick this time,"
said Old Porcupine.
    So Little Raccoon took a sturdy stick,
and walked back to the pool.
This time Little Raccoon held up his stick
and shook it.
But the thing in the pool had a stick, too.

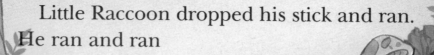

Little Raccoon dropped his stick and ran.
He ran and ran

past Fat Rabbit—

past Big Skunk—

past Old Porcupine—

and he did not stop till he was home.

Little Raccoon told his mother
all about the thing in the pool.
"I wanted to go for crayfish
all by myself," he said sadly.
"And you shall," said Mother Raccoon.
"Go back to the pool, Little Raccoon.
This time just smile.
Smile at the thing in the pool."

"Is that all?" asked Little Raccoon.
"Are you sure?"
    "I am sure," said his mother.
    Little Raccoon was brave
and his mother was sure.
So he went all the way back to the pool.

Little Raccoon made himself stand still.
He made himself look down.
Then he made himself smile at
the thing in the pool.
   The thing in the pool smiled back!
   Little Raccoon was so happy
he began to laugh.
The thing in the pool laughed, too.

"Now it wants to be friends," thought
Little Raccoon. "Now I can cross."

He ran to the other side of the pool
and began to dig.
Soon he had all the crayfish he wanted.

On his way back, he waved to the thing
in the pool.
The thing in the pool waved back.

Little Raccoon ran all the way home
with the crayfish.
   "This crayfish is so good,"
said his mother.
   "I can go alone any time now,"
said Little Raccoon.
"I'm not afraid of the thing
in the pool."
   "I know," said Mother Raccoon.

Little Raccoon looked at his mother.
"Tell me," he said.
"What *is* the thing in the pool?"
Mother Raccoon began to laugh.
Then she told him.